AF244462

Neon Hemlock Press
www.neonhemlock.com
@neonhemlock

Redundancies and Potentials
Dominique Dickey

Cover Design and Layout by Jordan Shiveley
Interior Design and Layout by dave ring
Edited by dave ring

Print ISBN-13: 978-1-952086-90-8
Ebook ISBN-13: 978-1-952086-91-5

Dominique Dickey
REDUNDANCIES & POTENTIALS
Neon Hemlock Press

NEON HEMLOCK

REDUNDANCIES AND POTENTIALS

BY DOMINIQUE DICKEY

For everyone who feels the future creeping up on them.
Hang on. We're gonna make it.

chapter ONE

"QUIGLEY IS A mindless corporate drone who's gotten into more trouble than he knows how to handle, and he made us to clean up his mess, which is objectively unfair," says Isadora, and she's right. I know she's right. But she's only saying that because we've been working all day and she's tired. I, for one, am still going to do the job that I was made to do, no matter how unfair it may be.

"I'm calibrating for twenty minutes forward," I say. "Time me." We're in Quigley's garage practicing our jumps. We have the whole house to ourselves, but we use the garage and the yard for messy work. There's three Isadora corpses stacked in the farthest corner. There's one or two of me crammed into the chest freezer. There's a pit of our component parts in the yard.

"Always," Isadora says.

"If I'm off by even a second, I need to know about it." I prefer it when Quigley times us—he's kinder about it—but he had to go into the office today, and he trusts us to handle ourselves.

"I know, I know," Isadora says. She's holding an old-fashioned stopwatch in one hand and a snub-nosed black pistol in the other. "And I guarantee you'll be off by more than just a second. You're not *that* good."

That comment is true, so I ignore it. "Headshot," I tell her. "One bullet."

"It's not like you'll fight me. It'll only take one shot."

"Even if I fight you. Even if I lose my nerve. I want it to be a headshot."

Isadora rolls her eyes. We've been over this a hundred thousand times, but it is the most important thing, to me. Agency rules dictate that only one version of a person can exist in the timeline—which means that redundant copies must be disposed of. The Agency doesn't dictate how that disposal must be handled, and some people are frankly awful about it. If I have to die—if a *version* of me has to die—I want that death to be as easy as possible. I deserve that, at least.

"Aster, are you going or not?"

"Fine. I'm gone."

My vision goes black. My pupils emit a burst of light, like a camera flash—I've seen it happen to Isadora enough times that I know what it looks like. There is a faint beeping from the implants in my skull, a sound that only I can hear. And then I am in the future.

It is twenty minutes and forty-two seconds later when I materialize in the wrong corner of the garage, on top of the pile of cold and stiff Isadora-bodies.

The living Isadora has her back to me and a machete
in her hand—where did she get a machete?—and she's
covered head to toe in blood.

My blood.

She turns to me as if surprised to have been caught.
I have never hated her more. I left her alone for twenty
minutes and forty-two seconds and she did *this*? She uses
her thumb to wipe gore off the face of the stopwatch.
"You're late," she says.

"I thought we agreed on a headshot."

She shrugs.

"You butchered me. Again."

"I eliminated a redundancy in accordance with
Agency standards," she says. The Agency *is* brutal about
eliminating redundancies.

"Fuck off and die."

"Hey, you get to kill me next."

"I don't enjoy killing you."

She shrugs again. "I enjoy killing you very much," she
says. "My turn. Twenty minutes forward. Time me."

Isadora hands me the pistol. Her eyes flash. I start
the timer. Her eyes return to their normal shade of shit
brown. She walks over to the pile of her bodies. I shoot
her cleanly between the eyes, pull out a folding chair, and
wait.

She is two whole minutes late.

THERE USED TO be this thing called a fax machine. It
would scan an original document and send the raw data
telephonically to another fax machine, where the data
would be converted back into visuals and printed. Boom,
two copies of the same document, existing in two different
places. Pretty neat, huh?

When the Agency cracked time travel, after nearly a century of experimentation, they called it TimeFax. It works just the same as a fax machine. People—the original documents, in this scenario—are scanned by a TimeFax machine, sent as raw data to another point in the timeline, and reconstituted by the recipient TimeFax machine. A duplicate of themself. Two copies of the same person, existing at two different points in time.

It took the Agency ninety-seven years to crack the original TimeFax. It took Quigley and Lowell eleven years to remix it, to create a series of cybernetic implants that allow someone to fax themself across time and space, from point A to point B, without a machine to send them off or to receive them. In short, that's what Prime is. That's what Isadora and I are.

We are paper that can fax itself.

Well, that sounded way cooler in my head.

Operating a TimeFax machine is so easy a kid could do it with one arm tied behind their back. You punch in two sets of coordinates—time and location—and then you're ready to go. You can go anywhere, forwards or backwards along the timeline, as long as there's a machine waiting to receive you.

The problem with TimeFax is that you can only bounce from machine to machine, from Agency office to Agency office, which limits where and when you can go.

The problem with being self-faxing, with using cybernetics to create pathways through time, is calibration.

Which is why we practice our jumps. Small increments, at first, then bigger ones, because error scales up. The job we were built for will take a pretty big jump, with a high degree of accuracy. When we jump, Isadora and I always land near each other in space, but there's a chance that I'll intercept her at the wrong point in the timeline.

TimeFax machines can go backwards, but we can't, and neither can Prime. It's a one way trip: overshoot the mark, and you're stuck in the future waiting for the world to catch up. The thought of jumping months too far, or even *years*, leaves me feeling frozen all over.

Isadora must feel the same cold, crawling dread—not that she'd ever say as much. It's probably why she keeps killing my duplicates in the most needlessly awful ways.

That, and my jumps being far more accurate than hers.

I try to explain my approach to her but I can tell she's not listening: "It's the opposite of time-blindness, right? You have to imagine thirty minutes passing, and then jump to the other side of it. Okay, imagine that your entire life is a rope under tension. Thirty minutes would be what, an inch? Visualize it passing through you, then jump."

"Are you going, or aren't you?" she asks.

"Headshot."

"Headshot," she says. The lying bitch.

A white flash, a low beep, and I'm gone.

THIRTY-ONE MINUTES LATER, she's holding my head in her hands. The smell of blood is everywhere, stronger than the late-summer sagebrush and the pit festering outside. "Close, but no cigar," she says.

"Isa, you can't keep—"

She raises the head towards me, holding it by a thick hank of hair and turning it. There *is* a bullet hole clean through the forehead, a spray of shattered bone out the back of the skull. "I did."

It's not the gangly corpse on the concrete, neck still pouring blood onto Isadora's shoes, that does me in. It's not the mouth, which looks like I died gearing up to ask a question. It's not even the gray chunks of brain matter matted in the dark curls. It's the act of looking at the back of my own head. I feel suddenly queasy, slick with sweat all over.

She underhands the head into the pile of bodies in the far corner. I don't watch it land. "I'll imagine thirty minutes of rope," she says before she jumps.

I get started on cleaning the garage—this is our last jump of the day, and Quigley should be home any minute. The head goes first, out to this week's mass grave in the yard, followed by the rest of the body. Then the version of me Isadora went at with the machete, even though the way she's broken the body down makes it impossible to haul it outside in one trip.

When I come back from dumping my left leg and what I suspect was once my tongue in the pit, Quigley's in the garage, leaning back against one of the walls. He's changed out of the suit he wore to the Los Angeles Agency office, into one of the long-sleeved polo shirts he's always wearing around the house. "Hey, kid," he says, holding his arms out for me.

"I'm all bloody," I complain, but I go anyway. He hugs me for a long time. "I'm down to forty-two seconds of error on a twenty-minute jump."

"And you'll do even better than that, I'm sure." He kisses the top of my head.

"*Dad*," I whine, frustrated that a win can't just be a win. I have to be twice as good in order to please him, because that's how the world treats him—and how it'll treat me. This isn't malice, Quigley says, but practice. Respect will always be an uphill fight for people who look like us.

"How soon's Isa back?" he asks.

I slump against him. I've cleaned up the worst of Isadora's mess, and there's no point in complaining about her to Quigley: he'd do anything for her. Quigley tells her, *When all of this is over, you'll have a real life.* He tells me, *Work hard, be good, and we'll see what you become.*

He tugs on my hair. "How soon, hmm?"

I take the stopwatch out of my pocket. "The goal is seven minutes."

The *goal*, because she's trying to do something that no metaphor can capture. Something that I suspect can't really be taught, but that Quigley is determined to teach her anyway.

I get started on Isadora's pile: a mess of freckled limbs, heads of white-blond hair tangled together. At least when she's dead her mouth doesn't look like she's tasting something bitter. She's bigger than me but I'm stronger than I look, and it's a short trip to the pit. The first body tumbles in. I think I should say something, but there's nothing to say.

I get back to the garage right as Isadora materializes like a bad visual effect, as if she's been cut into the reel of film between one frame and the next. She's three minutes early, overcorrected. She looks around, her face slack. Her mouth twists downward the way it always does, lately, when she sees me.

"Hey, kid," Quigley says, and I tell myself that it's nothing, that his voice doesn't sound *warmer* when he's looking at her.

"Father," Isa says, and she sounds happier, too.

Quigley wraps his arm around her shoulders and tugs her back towards the house. "It sounds like you've had a big day, huh?" He looks back towards me. "Aster, you can finish cleaning this up, can't you?"

"Sure thing, Dad," I say as the door shuts behind them.

I GET MOST of the bodies outside, leaving one of each of us tucked in the chest freezer, and I'm halfway through filling in the grave with Quigley's backhoe when Isadora comes out shouting that dinner's almost ready. I try to guess how long I've been at it before checking the stopwatch; I'm off by two minutes.

I shower the day's grime off and make it to the dining room with my hair still wrapped in a microfiber towel. Quigley's made spaghetti. Across the table, Isadora looks murderous—nothing new. Quigley sits at the table's head and looks back and forth at the two of us. "My girls," he says, and he sounds almost sad. He picks up his fork.

We eat in silence, hungry from a day of exertion—me and Isadora—and pushing papers—Quigley. When we're done, our father clears the plates and comes back to the table. He pushes his chair in, then stands behind it. "I'm going away," he says. I feel myself frown, and try to smooth it over. "On assignment. Fifty-two years forward—to stop the insurrection before it can happen. Do you get what that means? They've found Prime, found the right time and place to stop her, without even knowing that she's the one gumming up the works. I'm being sent ahead of you, and it's a good thing—there's something I need to build, something I don't have the tools for yet. The tools don't *exist* yet. I'll leave you instructions, coordinates. You'll keep practicing, and you'll come meet me when you're ready, and we'll save the world."

"You aren't coming back?" Isadora asks. When I look at her, she's chewing on her lip.

"You'll come to *me*," Quigley says. "That means you'll keep practicing your jumps on your own, and that means you'll have to be careful."

"Why can't you come back?" Her voice comes out so small that I have to remind myself she's grown, though she may not always act like it. And besides, we know why: backwards travel is rarely approved by the Agency. If you're sent forward on assignment, you're expected to adjust, to acclimate. To stay where they put you, until they see fit to send you somewhere else.

"Office politics. You'll be okay," Quigley says. He bends forward to kiss her forehead. I feel like he's speaking only to Isadora, like I'm eavesdropping. "I've made the toughest girls in the world—all you need is more practice. Keep each other accountable, work on your jumps, and—when you work your way up to longer increments, *be careful.* There's no need to be cocky, yeah? Keep each other safe."

I clear my throat. "When do you leave?"

Quigley braces his weight against the back of his chair. "Later tonight," he says. "Just…keep practicing while I'm gone, okay? I'll miss you. I'm counting on you."

chapter
TWO

QUIGLEY MADE PRIME in the basement of an Agency black site, brought her to life like an off-brand Dr. Frankenstein. She was a discarded double—but bringing her back to life was fair play, you see, because her original had died for good. And besides, she was hardly the same person, with a brain damaged from half a year on ice and loaded up with Agency cybernetics.

Cybernetics that Quigley had helped design in the first place, but that's beside the point.

The first question Prime asked: "Who am I?"

The second: "Where am I?"

And the third: "When am I?"

She'd only been awake for a few minutes. Quigley was still giving her the orientation to being reanimated, explaining that she could use TimeFax without…a TimeFax machine.

Her eyes flashed white and quick as he could say "oh, fuck" she'd spawned a duplicate somewhere else, somewhen else.

The problem is that there were no brakes on her, no reason for her not to skip off to whenever she felt like. And that's exactly what she did.

Quigley, loyal fool that he is, killed her not too long after that. There could only be one Prime fucking up the timeline, after all.

So he lost her. His greatest experiment, his most illicit creation, was gone.

And then Quigley made the two of us.

He's a bit of a one-trick pony, Quigley is. He followed the same procedure—Agency black site, discarded and frozen duplicate bodies, experimental cybernetics buried under the cold rot of our skin. The difference between us is that Prime was a singleton, and Isadora and I were made to be sisters. We land together, wherever and whenever we jump. We are drawn to each other through time. We are family.

And one of us can't up and disappear without the other. So we stuck around through the orientation to being undead, where Quigley explained that we have our old selves' personalities and proclivities, but only fragments of their memories. We made our first jumps together— seconds at a time into the future, landing in the garage with gunshots still ringing in the air and our duplicate bodies falling to the floor. We ate our meals with Quigley around the wooden table of his farmhouse. Isadora called him "Father" to his face, and by his name behind his back. I called him "Father" always, at first.

Then Quigley started to spend time with Isadora, without me. Then Isadora started to hate me, her mouth taking on that permanently angry cast. Then Quigley sifted through time to find Prime in the future, to assess the destruction she had wrought and inform us of how we were to undo it. Then Quigley went to the future for good, and left us alone to finish our training.

I WORK UP to jumping a whole day. Isadora is still working in increments of hours. I don't look forward to leaving her alone with a disposable iteration of myself for that long. I don't want to see what kind of mess I'll come back to.

She promises it'll just be a headshot.

She always promises that.

And then a day later I am in the garage, standing over a tied down copy of myself. Isadora kneels on the other side of the writhing body, her hand to my double's forehead as if she's checking for a fever. There is an odd tenderness in the gesture, given that my double is missing both arms and gray from blood loss.

She's still alive: I can tell from the spinning, unanchored feeling in my head and my gut. Temporal distortion. Quigley warned us about it—about what happens if two iterations of the same person overlap in the timeline—but I never experienced it before.

Isadora pulls the stopwatch from her pocket. "Right on time," she says. I am trying not to gag.

"You couldn't have wrapped all this up before I—"

"Mmmfpf," the other me says, and pain shoots through my temples. If the distortion is this bad for me, what must it be like for *her*?

"She doesn't have a tongue," Isadora explains.

"You sick bastard."

"I always start with the tongue," says Isadora. "Because you've got one smart mouth. Want me to tell you how I do it?"

I hold my hand out to her for the gun, tucked into the back of her baggy, bloodstained jeans. "Let me at least put her out of her misery."

"I say to you, I say— 'You can tolerate pain, and it's not like you're really dying. You have nothing to be afraid of. We're just gonna have a bit of fun, you and me.' And then I dig in with the knife."

"That's more than enough," I tell her. Isadora gives me the little black pistol.

"I'm sorry," I say to my double, before I execute her. Her blood—my blood—sprays warm onto my face. The blooming migraine dissipates.

I take the gun with me and head for the door to the house. "We're done for the day," I tell Isadora. "You can clean that up yourself."

WE KEEP PRACTICING. We get better. We start burning bodies, when we run out of places in the yard to bury them. I feel sick watching my doubles go up in flames. Isadora holds her hands out for warmth like it's a normal bonfire. We fight over dumb shit—whose turn it is to take out the trash, who left their hair in a snarl in the shower drain. Isadora can't handle conflict and takes it out on my doubles, torturing them in unique ways and always making sure I see. My hate for her grows like an organ, like a cancer. It is a hard knot right under my sternum, in front of my heart, where my love for her used to live.

I eliminate her doubles quickly, with the mercy and dignity they deserve. I don't even want to dismember her, no matter how awful she is to me.

I am gone for two years—my longest jump yet. When I reappear in the garage, she has the stopwatch in her hand and says, "Right on time."

"Where—"

"Already long dead, don't worry."

"Oh, thank *fuck*."

"Don't you want to know how I did it? I really outdid myself this time."

"I have a feeling you're going to tell me anyway."

"It was a headshot."

"Oh?" I'm headed towards the house now. Long jumps leave me feeling like there's a film on my skin and a hole in my belly, and I could do for a shower and a protein bar. I can still hear the beeping of the cybernetics in my skull.

"I made you beg," Isadora says, voice gone harsh.

"Okay." I really don't care for the how or why. The problem is that whether I bite or not, Isadora will say—

"I threatened to leave your double alive indefinitely, fucking up the timeline with multiple branching versions of you. Changes made to the duplicate are not reflected in the original, or whatever Agency bullshit Quigley used to say. *And* the temporal distortion would make your lives hell, both of you."

I know God isn't real, because no merciful god would let Isadora talk so damn much.

"She felt so guilty that she begged to be put down," says Isadora. "And I guess that's why you're perfect for this job. Why you were *made* for this job. Just like our buddy Quigley, you'll do whatever the Agency tells you to do."

I don't bother answering. I have a hard time imagining myself—any version of myself—begging to die. I'd always thought of myself as more likely to run, or try and fight back in a moment of panic, especially knowing the terrible things that Isadora would do to me. I do what Quigley says because I trust him, but our orders don't come from the Agency. Agency employees are trained to embrace death, to crave it where it rights the timeline. The two of us don't have that training—at least, not in our functioning memories. Not these versions of ourselves.

We spend a week together, the silences between us tense. Isadora has shifted all the furniture and rearranged the kitchen. I keep stubbing my toes and I can't remember for the life of me where the spoons go.

Then it is Isadora's turn to jump—six months, and she's frustrated with her slow progress, but it's not like she ever listens to my advice. We go out to the garage.

Her eyes flash. I start the stopwatch. She hands me the pistol. I put it down on the chest freezer. "Not yet. Go in the house."

"What?"

"I'm not killing you. Not yet."

"I gathered as much. What I'm trying to figure out is why."

"Go inside," I say, but Isadora picks up the pistol and shoots herself through the temple. Great.

I spend half a year alone. When Isadora comes back, I tell her I *made* her double kill herself. I don't tell her how I was bested, how I was lonely, how I was outdone.

Isadora's next jump is a whole year forward. Just before she jumps, I put the gun in Quigley's safe and change the passcode. We go out to the garage. Her eyes flash. I start the stopwatch.

"You have the pistol?" she asks.

"Go in the house," I tell her.

"You're gonna kill me *inside*?"

"Go in the house."

"Okay, Aster, I'm confused."

"I'm not going to kill you. Not yet. And if you don't buy Quigley's Agency bullshit like you say you don't, you won't kill yourself, either."

Isadora grits her teeth. "Is this about when I moved all the furniture two inches to the left? Because that was just funny."

"I'm not punishing you. I'm testing you. Go inside."

I LIVE WITH the throwaway version of Isadora for three hundred and sixty-two days before I put her down, and I swear we almost become friends. Isadora's angry mouth relaxes, and I start to see how soft her face can be. She chews on her lip when she's concentrating. She remembers how to bake bread without a recipe. She likes pulpy crime dramas. She knows a lot about cigars.

The two of us were discarded bodies, pulled from the morgue and resurrected, outfitted with Quigley's stolen cybernetics. No relation—at least, not that we know of—but he insisted on calling us sisters. For those three hundred and sixty-two days I spend with Isadora's double, I think I see how we could become sisters, how we could love each other. How we could be how we used to be.

But that's not the story, not really. That's far from the most important thing that happens in those three hundred and sixty-two days. No—for nearly a year, I'm haunted, and I don't know who's haunting me.

chapter
THREE

WHEN WE WERE brand new, before she turned against me, Isadora used to sleep in my bed. She was afraid, though she'd never admit it—and who could blame her? She'd been brought back from the dead in Quigley's lab with no idea who she was, pointed towards a target and made to fire. Her life's work was to stop an insurrection that had yet to happen, an insurrection hardly anyone knows anything about. Of course she was scared.

She would sneak into my room and sit at the foot of my bed, just *staring* at me, until I startled awake. "Come on," I'd say, tugging back the blankets and shifting to make room for her. "If you're coming, come on."

She wouldn't say anything, just curl up at the edge of the mattress and fall fast asleep in a matter of seconds.

Once she was out, she was out hard—nothing could wake her until morning. All she ever needed was an invitation.

THE HAUNTING STARTS when I'm in the shower. Isadora's left a clump of white-blond hair stuck to the tile wall below the faucet and I'm trying to think of something appropriately passive-aggressive to say about it when I get that feeling again, like I'm spinning end over end. Sharp, bright pain—a pickaxe through my temple.

I turn the water off, even though half of my body's still covered in soap, and keel forward against the shower wall, now eye-level with Isadora's disgusting clump of hair, which only makes me feel more sick.

I don't know how long I stand there gasping—time goes slippery in my grip—but I know that the feeling recedes as instantly as it began. Weird. I turn the water back on, wait for it to run hot, and flick the blond tangle into the drain.

And honestly, I don't think much of it, until I step out the shower and see what's written in the steam on the mirror: *DO YOU KNOW WHO YOU ARE?*

IT'S A FULL week after the shower incident when I feel a weight settle at the end of my mattress. "Come on, if you're coming," I mumble, feeling like time is echoing around me.

A flare of pain through the top of my skull wakes me quickly. The weight at the end of the bed shifts. I reach for the bedside lamp.

It's *not* Isadora. It's someone with brown skin, wearing navy blue coveralls, with a black plastic bag pulled down over their head. Perfectly still, not even breathing. The body slides bonelessly off the end of the mattress to land on the floor with a *thump*. I flinch, hoping Isadora is soundly asleep across the hall, before I climb out of bed and tear the plastic bag open with blunt fingernails.

It's my face. My own eyes, bloodshot and vacant, look back at me.

I STARE AT the body for a long time, uncomprehending, until a plan begins to form—slowly, the way a frying egg sets around the edges. First, I check the body's pockets. Empty. Then, I strip the coveralls off; the long zip down the front makes it easy.

There's a scrap of yellow paper tucked in the gray sports bra, damp around the edges with sweat but still legible: *DO YOU KNOW WHO YOU ARE?* I stash it under my pillow and search the body for any identifying marks: scars, tattoos, piercings. I know it's me—it has to be, or else I wouldn't have had that flash of temporal distortion in the shower and again tonight—but from *when?*

Well, if she's made it here without a TimeFax machine, then she's from somewhere in the past. And her jumps are surgically precise, and she knows exactly where to find me.

I have an ugly scar up the center of my knee, thick and shining red against the smooth brown of my skin, with little dots to either side where the sutures must have gone in. It aches when I wake up, especially if the weather's cold. Pain is one of those things that gets easy to ignore with time.

When I peel her out of the coveralls, she has the same scar, but it doesn't catch the light the same way. It's duller, softer in both texture and color. Looks like it doesn't hurt at all.

Well, there are plenty of explanations for that. Maybe she gets acupuncture, or uses some kind of fancy scar cream. I don't think too hard about it. Mostly I'm thinking about killing her for good, because I am supposed to be the *only* me. But to kill her, I have to catch her—and catch her alive.

I tip the bare body over my shoulder and carry it downstairs, still raw with sleep, tired enough for my eyes to itch. I figure I'll take it out to the property line, farther out than we usually bury bodies, where I should be able to dig without hitting bones. I grab a shovel from the garage and trek across Quigley's acreage with a small flashlight held in my teeth.

I have to take a couple breaks, and my pajamas are soaked through with sweat by the time I make it to the row of pine trees that marks the property's edge. I sit with my back against a tree trunk for as long as it takes to catch my breath—longer than I'd like. I haven't buried a body in two months and I'm losing muscle mass, or aerobic capacity; I can never remember which one is the first to go.

It's a cool night, early spring, the air thick with pine and the smog floating up toward us from Los Angeles. Something heavy hides underneath that, with the sweetness of rot. Like the mass graves we used to dig for our smaller jumps, covered with tarps for days on end until Quigley decided it was time to fill them in. Bodies packed tightly together, being eaten from the inside out by their own microbes, from the outside in by birds and worms.

It's not a *bad* smell, not exactly, but it clings to everything it touches. It's the kind of smell that lingers.

I get up and start digging. The grave isn't especially deep—not my best work—but the body rolls in all the same. The sky is starting to lighten when I'm done filling in the hole. I turn the flashlight off, stretch, and pace back and forth along the row of trees a few times, thinking: *do* I know who I am?

I know what I'm *for*, and that should be enough. I'm here to practice my jumps until I'm good enough, to stop an insurrection that would kneecap the Agency before it can start, to anchor Isadora in the timeline as she anchors me. And if I can figure out why she's been so mean lately, well, that would be a nice bonus. I know all I need to know.

The sun keeps rising, and I'm maybe twenty yards from the grave I just filled in when I see it: a navy blue lump tucked between two trees. The sweet-stale smell intensifies as I go towards it.

Another me, dressed in the same coveralls, dead for days and crawling with maggots.

Looks like I'm digging another hole.

When I finally make it back upstairs, light's coming buttery-yellow through the window at the end of the hallway and Isadora's bedroom door is still closed. I shower and start a load of laundry—the machines are in the unfinished basement, though I'm given to understand that basements are rare in California. Then I crawl back into bed, set on making up the hours of sleep that were stolen from me.

I'm drifting off when I remember the scrap of paper I tucked away under my pillow. I reach for it, halfway making sure it's still there, and my fingertips brush against something else—still paper but stiffer, thicker.

I sit up and shove the pillow off the bed altogether.

There's the little note: *DO YOU KNOW WHO YOU ARE?*

There's a glossy brochure with the Agency logo: **THE POTENTIALS AND YOU.**

And there's a stapled zine that looks like it was run off on a home printer: **WE DETERMINE OUR OWN POTENTIAL**.

chapter FOUR

AN IDEA IS a funny thing: some sink in fast and some take hold over time. They all come to the same end.

My duplicate is trying to tell me something, and I am determined not to listen, but she's got her hooks in me. This one will be slow. Inevitable.

Isadora asks me to put active dry yeast in our grocery order. "Just a hunch," she says. "A feeling. What's it to you?" But then a few days later she's made a loaf of bread from scratch and now I'm wondering if *she* knows who *she* is. I sure as hell don't.

It wears on me, gets to be too much to bear.

At least the bread is good.

I READ THE brochure first. *A natural consequence of TimeFax is the proliferation of redundancies*, it begins. *All redundancies must be disposed of in accordance with Agency guidelines. This ensures that we can continue to use TimeFax to protect our communities, and better the lives of future generations.* Familiar. The same shit Quigley's always talking about. The Agency started as a private police force, offering protection to anyone willing to pay for it—corporations, mostly. TimeFax has always been just another tool in their arsenal.

The next page is a diagram, with **REDUNDANCIES** in one column and **POTENTIALS** in the other. There's some jargon I don't understand, but I think I can see the shape of it. A point that's so worn in, it barely has to be articulated.

You start by creating duplicates of people, then implementing monitoring systems to make sure those duplicates don't spread too far. Putting redundancies down like dogs. Using them for target practice. I think of Isadora with her machete, carving me open.

And from there, there's just *so much else* you could do with those same monitoring systems. So many *other people* you can put down like dogs, use for target practice, carve open with a sharp knife. Once you're already committing murder on that scale, it's not much of a stretch to start paring off civilians too.

The first step—the most important step—is to put a label on them. Tell the world that they cause more trouble than they're worth, that we don't need them anyway. Scan the timeline for crimes that they *could* commit, then call them potential criminals.

The last page: *If you or someone you know is deemed a potential, please dial the following number and/or report to your local Agency office.*

I fold the brochure back up along the crisp lines in the thick paper, then tear the whole thing in half. No way of knowing when it's from. No way of knowing what my double expects me to do about it, what she wants from me.

Whatever game she's playing here, I'm not in it.

QUIGLEY'S BEDROOM DOOR has been closed since he left. "Come on," Isadora says, as she washes flour off her forearms in the kitchen sink. "Let's watch a movie, or something."

There's a flatscreen TV at the end of Quigley's unmade bed. We sprawl out in sheets that smell more like dust than like him. It's been a long time.

Isadora tucks her cold feet under my calf and thumbs through options until she finds a heist movie. "I…think I remember this one," she says.

"Oh?"

She shrugs, pulls her lower lip between her teeth. "Just a feeling."

We're an hour in and either her feet have warmed up or I've stopped noticing the cold when she says, "Her husband isn't dead."

"Bullshit." We saw the lead's husband die in the opening scene.

"He's not! Watch."

Sure enough, Isa's spoiled the plot twist. She looks extraordinarily pleased with herself by the time the credits roll. "Just a good guess," I say. I've never been the best at seeing the shape of a story from a distance.

"I *remembered*."

And there it is again: she knows who she is, who she was. Her past life. I *don't*, and I've got a double who's determined to rub it in.

Isadora turns to reruns of a crime show, decades old, the video quality fuzzy. She's snoring before the episode's halfway through, like the quiet safety of it's lulled her right to sleep: Quigley's big bed, her limbs barely touching mine.

I think about smothering her—I bet I could get my weight on her chest, a pillow over her slack face, before she woke up enough to react. But that's not really what I want; I'd still have nine lonely, haunted months. Better to suffer with her than without.

I leave her there and go back to my room, where I get the zine down from the top shelf in my closet. It's a compilation of obituaries, accompanied by grainy black and white photographs of the dead. Aaron Drake, age eighty-five. Kendra Emmerson, age fifty. Evan Cryan, age twenty-two. Miranda Tapping, age eleven. Carlos Fuller, age six. The names and faces keep going, going.

The last page: **REMEMBER WHO THE AGENCY TOOK FROM US.**

The logical outcome of the brochure, though there's no way of knowing how much time passed between the two pieces of ephemera. No way of knowing when either of them is from, how the past and future will unfold to make these events true.

I tuck the zine back into its place in the closet. I lay down on the floor at the foot of my bed, my arms folded over my chest like I'm in a coffin. There is another me bopping around the timeline, fucking things up, fucking with me. That simply cannot be.

I want her dead.

But first, I have questions for her.

A LONG TIME ago, I woke to the feeling of Isadora's weight settling at the foot of my bed. "Come on," I said, making room for her, but she shook her head and held her arms out for me. Her hair was a mess and, even though I was below her, something about the gesture made her look like a child asking to be picked up.

I sat up, not even half awake. "Fine. Well, come *here*." She tucked herself against my chest and went still, like she was just listening to my heartbeat through my shirt, one hand forming a fist in the back of it. I could feel her breathing. I could tell she was afraid. I dozed like that, I don't know for how long.

When she pulled herself up and kissed me my first thought was *What the fuck?* but my second thought was *Oh, I guess that's funny* and then my third thought was *What the fuck!?* again, but louder this time.

"None of this is real," she said, her mouth still too close to mine. "This home, this family."

"I—"

"Don't worry, I just wanted to see what you'd do."

"What the fuck." I was thinking it so loudly, I felt like she was bound to hear it either way.

She laughed: the sound rattled in her chest at first, then came out loudly enough that I was worried she'd wake Quigley.

"You'll wake Dad," I said, but that only made her laugh louder, harder. That might have been the last time I heard her laugh with real joy, without anger under the surface. It made her sound young, fragile.

"He's not our father," she said.

"We owe everything to him." We were bodies in the morgue. We could have died for good, stayed dead.

"We're *tools*." Still, she sounded elated by the fact. "We're going to save the world."

I fell back against the pillows and waited her out, waited for the giggle fit to end. Still laughing, she dug her fingers in on either side of my waist. Like she was measuring me for a dress in her head; like she was developing an aptitude for remembering and replicating volume, instead of time.

"We're going to save the world," she repeated, somber this time.

"Do you want to sleep here, or not?"

She leaned down over me and kissed me again—my forehead, this time. "If I ever get lost," she said, "come and find me."

"I always will," I promised. We anchor each other. We're a matched set.

When she crossed the hallway to her own bedroom, both doors slammed shut behind her.

chapter FIVE

'M HAVING A hard time sleeping and, really, who can blame me? I lay still and quiet and wound-up with anxiety until my heart beats so fast I feel like I'll faint. I never remember going unconscious—not until I'm waking up to the beeping of my alarm, almost the same tone and cadence as the beep of the cybernetics, and I'm *tired*.

The morning after we watch the heist movie, Isadora makes breakfast sandwiches on thick slices of bread. We eat in the dining room, where there's still a placemat at the head of the table. I think about Quigley, wonder what he would have me do.

I go for a run, taking laps of the property at a slow pace. I lift weights in the basement. I tear the zine into tiny strips of paper, then try eating them. All it does is suck the moisture from my mouth. I give up and toss the shreds into the trash instead.

I'm afraid to shower. I'm afraid to sleep. I'm afraid.
My double makes me wait.

A MONTH PASSES, and Isadora starts smoking cigars. I'm
guessing she's a real snob about it based on our joint
credit card statement. As long as she keeps this new habit
confined to the back porch, I don't care much. I imagine
her as a magician pulling rabbits out of a hat, except the
hat is her past and the rabbits are relics.

What does that make me? The magician's assistant, waiting
patiently to get sawed in half? I don't like this metaphor.

Anyway, it's a month later and I'm half asleep, drifting
off listening to the rapid thump of my own heart, when
a weight settles at the end of my mattress. I jackknife up,
hands raised and ready to swing.

Her pale hair catches what little light comes through
the window. She smells like smoke. "Sorry," Isadora says.
"For startling you. Sorry."

"Jesus Roosevelt Christ." I feel like my heart is vibrating
instead of beating. Ineffectual little movements in my chest,
as twitchy on the inside as I am on the outside.

It's been a long month.

"Isa, you can't—" She can't be here, she *can't*, because
what if my double chooses tonight to show up?

She reaches across my body to flick on the lamp on the
bedside table. The bulb warms up slowly. It's a long moment
before I've got enough light to see how scared she is, how
tightly she's holding herself together. Her eyes are red.

"Can I?" she asks. "Sleep here. Can I sleep here?"

I turn the lamp off, shove the duvet back. "Come on, if
you're coming."

Her breathing steadies as soon as her head hits the
pillow.

ANOTHER MONTH GOES by, and Isadora's the only one crawling into my bed. Not every night, but I'm terrified every time. It takes me too long to get back to sleep. I wonder if it's possible to lose your mind from slow sleep deprivation, or if I'm just learning to do without.

I run laps of the property. I lift weights in the basement. I sift the shreds of the zine out of my bedroom trash can and think about eating them for real, getting all of those names and faces inside of me. Carrying their stories, those lives cut short.

Isadora bakes bread and makes increasingly elaborate sandwiches. She tries to explain the differences between cigar shapes to me. She dozes off watching NCIS reruns in Quigley's bed four nights out of every seven.

I read the books on Quigley's shelves, fill my head with newness to make up for the old stories I'll never know.

I miss him. I wait.

SHE CATCHES ME in the middle of the afternoon. Isadora's on a sourdough kick: she's named her starter Quigley Jr. and she uses it in everything. Today it's cinnamon rolls, the warm smell floating down into the basement even though the door is closed.

I bought a used rowing machine on Craigslist and I'm halfway through a sprint when my ears start ringing. Pain digs down through the top of my skull. I grab a jump rope from a hook on the wall and manage to wrap an end around each of my hands, pulling the slack tight between them as I wheel around.

There she is. My face, my hair pulled into two buns.

Dark blue coveralls, unzipped just enough to show the top of her gray sports bra.

I'm coming at her with the makeshift garrote, trying to get her before—

Her eyes flash, and every step closer to her magnifies the echoing feeling in my head. If I can just get to the gun safe on the opposite wall—

But I've already lost this bout, and Isadora would hear the shot. That's no good. I can hardly think.

"I don't mind if you kill me," she says, "but I don't think that's what you really want."

"What do I want?"

"Hmm?"

"You're *me*, so tell me: what do I want?"

Her hands fall open at her sides. She sits down on the concrete floor. "To talk," she says.

"How am I supposed to—" I'm thinking it might be better for her to off herself, after all, and spare me this.

How is she still—

"How are you—?"

She laughs. I expect her to offer something condescending—*poor baby*, maybe, or *you'll just have to get used to it*. It catches me off guard when she says, "I know. It must be awful for you. Why don't you turn around? It's easier if you can't see me."

"I don't trust you," I grit out.

She stands up and strips methodically, kicking her clothes to the side, until she's just in her underthings. "Now?"

Isadora's voice cascades down through the floorboards: "Aster! Come get one while they're still warm!"

"Just a second!" I call back. My double smiles at me. I scowl at her. "Don't make me have to carry your corpse up the basement stairs."

"Cross my heart and hope to die," she says.

"This isn't finished," I say.

"I'm unarmed. I know you changed the passcode to the gun safe. Lock me in, if it makes you feel better." There *is* a deadbolt on the door at the top of the steps.

Still, I clumsily hogtie her with the jumprope before I go upstairs.

"THEY'RE STILL TOO hot to eat, but I know you'll want to shower first," Isadora says from the kitchen, and she's *right*, and it's jarring. I'm getting soft, getting used to this version of her. Getting used to her acting like she likes me.

I shower off and when I come downstairs, there's a glazed cinnamon roll and a cup of coffee in my place at the dining table. Isadora sits opposite me, her mug folded between her hands, her empty plate still in front of her.

"Couldn't wait, sorry," she says, and I shrug before taking a bite.

"Oh, that's *good.*"

"Right? I'm getting another." She takes her plate to the kitchen, comes back, sits down. We eat together quietly. "Want more? There's plenty left."

"I don't want to ruin my appetite for dinner."

"Theoretically, this *can* be dinner," she says. Conspiratorial, like we're kids left home alone. We *are*.

"I guess Dad's not here to stop us."

She's made six cinnamon rolls and we eat them all in one sitting, and the sugar has me feeling slow and heavy. And the sleep deprivation, I suppose, but I hope that's coming to an end now.

It occurs to me, then, that my double in the basement could just jump again—a short jump, seconds forward— and untie herself. I'm almost too full to care, and I suspect that temporal distortion would just make me extravagantly sick at this point. I'm not interested in seeing the cinnamon rolls come back up.

My eyes have gone unfocused and I'm halfway asleep at the table when Isadora says, "Come on, let's go watch something." I follow her upstairs to Quigley's room.

She puts on a police procedural and lays down with her legs resting against mine. She looks at me for a long, long time.

"It hurts me, too," she says. "Having to act so—but I couldn't kill you, if I didn't."

I swallow. I'm so close to just letting myself doze off. "Then why are you being nice to me now?"

"Because this version of me won't have to kill you again."

I don't tell her about the double tied up in the cellar. She's in a good mood, and why ruin it?

For the first time in weeks, I fall soundly asleep.

chapter SIX

W HEN I WAKE up, the room is dark and the TV is glowing blue. Isadora's still asleep, her breathing coming slow, her hair falling into her face. We have months left but it occurs to me that I'm going to miss her. I'm going to miss this.

I take the basement stairs backwards. "Oh, thank *god*," my own voice says from behind me.

She was right—I'm still dizzy but it's bearable. "You said I wanted to talk," I say. "So, talk."

"How much do you know about Prime?" she asks.

"How much do *you* know about Prime?"

"Oh, fuck off—"

"Fine!" I snap. The mental image of her face pinched up with frustration is almost endearing. "She was our dad's— Quigley's—first experiment. She's going to start a war. She's what we're here for." We're the cops, the cleanup crew.

Taking out Prime is our mission. I snap back into focus: this is all I need to know; anything more is a distraction.

Years from now, Isadora and I are going to kill her. We are going to save the world.

"Whose world are you saving?" the voice behind me asks.

"There's only one."

"Quigley's? The Agency's?" The voice sounds…closer. *"There's only one."*

A hand lands on my shoulder. The touch feels heavy, like it'll tug me down into the center of the planet. I'm not quite afraid to look, but I'm afraid of the spinning feeling. I'm afraid of how it'll hurt.

What was it that Isadora said? *You can tolerate pain.* I can, but maybe not like this.

"Surely you knew you could've untied yourself," she says. "And the new passcode—far too easy to guess."

"Don't—"

"I'm just sorry you'll have to clean this up," she says.

"Don't!" I'm halfway turned towards her when she shoots herself through the mouth.

It's a hell of a mess, and I curse the whole way through cleaning it up. I bury her at the property line. I change the safe's passcode again. I mop the basement, then mop again.

Isadora sleeps through it all. When I finally make it to bed, it's well after sunup and I hear her shuffling around.

I am trying to keep a firm grasp on the facts of the situation, but the truth is that I'm being made a fool of. There's only so much I can take.

I miss Quigley. I miss feeling like big decisions weren't mine to make. He'd know what to do, what to say.

But he trusts us—though I suspect he trusts Isadora more than me—and we'll see him again. Our jumps will get longer and we'll chew through time and meet him on the other side. Soon.

When I wake, well into the afternoon, Isadora makes me sourdough pancakes with batter left over from her breakfast. "The secret's in Quigley Jr.," she says, patting the mason jar of starter. I have to remind myself that she isn't the real Isadora, the one I'll be stuck with once all of this is done. I wonder what I'll do with the starter after I have to kill her.

I have never liked killing her, never taken the kind of savage joy in it that she finds in killing me, but I can tell already that this one will be different. This one will hurt because this Isadora—my friend—will be replaced by the version of her that hates me.

It's quite possible that I've made a series of tactical errors. It's quite possible that I've been wrong-footed from the start.

"I miss Quigley," I say.

She snorts, grabs a Sharpie from the junk drawer. "We can pretend he's still here." She draws a happy face on the glass jar of starter, a few points of stubble along the jaw— turns out drawing isn't one of the talents she's uncovered. A speech bubble: *I've made the toughest girls in the world.*

THAT NIGHT, ISADORA'S sacked out in my bed and I'm finding it impossible to get back to sleep. The distortion creeps in slowly, fuzz around the edges of things. I keep my eyes pointed toward the ceiling.

"Bed's already too crowded," I say, imagining her appearing at the foot of it, stitched into the film reel. I don't have to see her to know what it looks like.

Still, she perches on the corner of the mattress next to my feet. Isadora's breathing is as sleep-steady as ever.

"What else do you know about Prime?" she asks.

"She's my mission." I hear her suck in a breath, about to speak. "Don't ask me whose world I'm saving."

"Fine. Let me put it this way: whose side are you on?"

"What the fuck kind of question is that?"

Again, I don't have to see her to picture her shrugging. She's me, after all.

"Okay, whose side are *you* on?" I ask.

"Sit up, and I'll tell you."

Right now, the dizziness is a dull roar. She wants me to make it worse—on purpose—before she'll play ball.

Well, maybe if I close my eyes, it won't be so bad. I push myself up and I can't feel just how close she is until—

She kisses me and my first thought is *What the fuck?* but my second thought is *Oh, I guess that's funny*, and it's the second thought that really counts in a situation like this.

My third thought is *What the fuck!?* but louder, and my fourth thought is *Ouch*, because I feel it now: pain through my temples.

"What the fuck," I whisper. On the other side of the double bed, Isadora snores wetly.

My double slides smoothly backwards off the bed, then pushes the window at the foot of it open. She's got one leg over the ledge when she says, "Look under your pillow."

It's a short drop, and I don't hear her hit the ground. What I *do* hear, seconds later, is a shot.

Isadora makes a snuffling sound into the pillow, but doesn't wake.

I'M GETTING GOOD at burying my own body in the dark.

Eight nights in a row. "I'm awake," I say, when the spinning feeling starts.

"Keep your eyes closed," she tells me, before she tucks something under my pillow and slides out the window. Two times, Isadora's in my bed and stays fast asleep.

What does she leave me? Three zines (**WE DETERMINE OUR OWN POTENTIAL**); three notes (*DO YOU KNOW WHO YOU ARE? DO YOU KNOW WHO PRIME IS? DO YOU KNOW WHO LOWELL WAS?*); a Polaroid of Quigley looking much younger in what I assume is a lab; a Polaroid of *me* looking professional in a collared dress, hair pulled into a neat chignon.

Both photos are candid, the subject not quite looking into the camera—focused on the whole rest of their life, waiting just out of frame.

It's not a memory, not quite, but a *suspicion*: we took the photos of each other. He knew me, before I was myself.

chapter SEVEN

O N THE NINTH night, she's reaching to slide her hand under my pillow when I catch her around the wrist. The distortion is debilitating, but I breathe through it. "Wait."

She freezes. "I'll stay," she says. She frees herself from my grip in a quick motion, then vaults over my body to what I've come to think of as Isadora's side of the bed. She's sitting facing me, her legs tucked underneath herself. I mirror her.

"I don't like that you're in my bed in your outside clothes," I say. I have no idea where those coveralls have been. "Now I'll have to change the sheets. Happy?"

"*That's* what's getting you about all this?"

"It's incredibly inconsiderate of you."

She makes a face. I recognize it from the mirror. I clear my throat before I ask, "Are you the one that kissed me?"

"I haven't yet, but I'm close enough to count."

"Why?"

She laughs softly, sadly. "You don't remember your own sense of humor," she says. "God, he really fucked you over."

And I'm caught in the gut by it, by how much I don't know about myself. "I was frozen. For a really long time, okay? I—"

"Okay, okay, it wasn't your dad that did it, it was the ice, sure—wait, does he really make you call him *dad*?"

"He's…my father." I miss him so terribly.

Another expression I recognize: she's trying not to roll her eyes. Failing. "I think this is the part where I shoot myself."

"Can you at least go out to the pine trees first?" It'll save me having to carry the body.

She undoes the latch on the window, then looks back at me.

"Are you ever going to tell me who Prime is?" I ask her. I don't need to know. I shouldn't know—Quigley would've told me, if it was relevant to my purpose.

But I *want* to know. The wanting feels like something slimy in my gut, or maybe that's just the temporal distortion.

Her eyebrows tilt downwards. "Oh, sweetheart," she says, and then she's walking back towards the bed. She touches my face. It hurts, and it doesn't. "What do you think I've been trying to do?"

She climbs out the window. A few minutes later, a distant shot.

Isadora knocks. Strange—she's never knocked before. "Hey, did you hear that?"

"Must've been the neighbors. A coyote, maybe." The nearest neighbor is half a mile away, but she believes me: I can hear her slippers shuffling back across the hall to her bedroom. "Goodnight!" I call. Her door slams.

She must not have been asleep, not really. She can sleep through anything.

A close call. Too close.

I BURY THE body, shower, strip the sheets off my bed, then start to feel slow and tired right after I've got the bedding in the washing machine. I lay down on the couch in the living room—*just for a minute*, I tell myself, but then it's morning and Isadora's kneading dough at the kitchen counter, a smudge of flour obscuring the dark freckles on her pale face.

"I was thinking cinnamon rolls again," she says, and I agree, then run the sheets through the washer again in case they've gone mildewy from sitting wet.

Last night's trophy from my double is on the shelf in my closet where I've left it: a Polaroid of me and Quigley, our heads bowed close together over a microscope, his hand resting on my hip. I'm smiling at him, even as my body tilts away from his.

There is no caption, no date.

I HAVE NEVER been the best at seeing the shape of a story from a distance.

She's trying to tell me something, but it's going right over my head. Like Isadora guessing—*remembering*—the plot twists in basically every movie we watch together. The kind of thing that makes you feel really stupid when it finally clicks.

On the tenth night, Isadora is asleep beside me and I've got my eyes squeezed tightly shut. "I'm listening," I say, "but you're going to have to explain very slowly, in lots of small words."

She makes a sound like she's trying not to laugh. "Oh. Sweetheart, *oh*."

I feel my ears go red. At least it's dark. I'm curled toward the edge of the bed, and she sits in the space made by my body.

"Are you going to blame the time on ice for this?" she asks me, but it's kind—like I'm in on the joke, not the butt of it.

"Maybe," I say, not sure if I'm allowed to laugh. If laughing would break this.

"You got a marker? Maybe it'll help if I label this one for you."

"Downstairs. First drawer on the right when you go in the kitchen."

She leaves my bedroom door open but she doesn't come back, and I don't go looking for her until after I've heard the gunshot.

She's left a Polaroid on the kitchen counter, next to Quigley Jr: me and Quigley. I'm bent towards a microscope and he's behind me, his arms around me, both of my wrists held in one of his hands. She's drawn exaggerated devil horns over his head. In the white space at the bottom of the photo, she's written *Q + LOWELL*.

WHEN I BURY her, I dump everything she's ever given me in the grave.

SHE LEAVES ME alone for three months.

chapter EIGHT

'VE TAKEN TO reading Quigley's books in the garage with the big door open, letting in a rectangle of sunlight. Every time I look up, I expect to see him, sitting in his chair in the corner like he used to watch us. We had the unsteady and malleable minds of infants, after all that time on ice before he brought us back. He would chew his thumbnails and time our jumps. He would kill our duplicates kindly. He wasn't nearly old enough to have fathered us, but he treated us like we were his responsibility—a responsibility he never resented, because we were part of a larger puzzle. We were a means to an end.

He took care of us.

He lied to us, but doesn't any good father lie?

It's an unreasonably humid day, hot even in the shade of the garage door, when Isadora comes out and sits next to me. "Mind if I smoke?" she asks.

"Your funeral."

She methodically lights her cigar, rotating the clipped end over a long wooden match. I watch her hands, her face. She pulls her lip between her teeth.

It's occurred to me to ask her—of *course* it's occurred to me to ask her—but it always seemed like a terrible idea. I don't hate her. I don't *want* to hate her. Her answer, no matter what it is, will make me hate her.

And besides, who's to say she wouldn't lie? Just to twist the knife, the fact that she knows something I don't.

I think of her in Quigley's bed, her legs folded around mine: *I couldn't kill you if I didn't.* That other her, the real her, is putting on a face. Acting cruel because that's the only way for her to *be* cruel.

That doesn't make it hurt any less. That doesn't make me trust her any more.

She brings the cigar to her lips. I breathe in deep—so much humidity I think I'll drown where I'm sitting, the acidic stink of tobacco—before I ask her: "What do you know about Prime?"

"Oh."

"*Oh?*"

Smoke curls out of her open mouth, drifts away. "It's just, the other me would be so *angry.*"

Does that really matter? Does any of that matter, when I'm real—right here—and angry in the present? I'm not some hypothetical.

"He told you who she is," I say.

"The other me believes in him."

"And you *don't?*"

"I...do. He promised me a future."

"But?"

"I believe in you, too," she says. A perfect deflection, like my double calling me *sweetheart.*

"Oh, I could kill you."

"What, two months?" she asks, waving her hand like she's brushing me off. A wisp of smoke follows the motion. She turns toward me, leans forward over her knees. "Will you do it yourself, or will you leave it up to me?"

"Sometimes," I say, as if that will soften anything. As if she deserves that little bit of mercy. "Sometimes, I absolutely despise you."

I go inside, shower until I'm sure the smell of smoke is out of my hair.

When she crawls into my bed that night, I mumble, "Come on, if you're coming."

She makes pancakes the next morning, as if it never happened.

TWO NIGHTS LATER I'm alone in my bed and then I'm not. My duplicate asks, "Are you ready?"

"For what?"

"To put the pieces together."

I drag my hands down over my face. Stretch the orbits of my eyes, the downward contour of my mouth. "Fuck. You."

"Am I meant to take that as a negative?" The mattress dips as she moves, then bounces back as she stands. The latch on the window clicks.

I sit up. The back of my head, hair in two buns. Navy blue coveralls. A spinning, sinking, aching feeling. "Okay, wait."

She turns towards me. She smiles.

"I'm Lowell," I whisper. It's the first time I've said it out loud: I'm the woman who worked with Quigley to devise the cybernetics. I was a genius, once. A firecracker.

And now I'm…me. This fractured mind is all that I have left.

"And?" she prompts.

"Quigley. He and I were…I don't know. I don't know this part."

"He was using you," she says. "For access. He's always been a climber, that one."

"Always?" It's just that my head hurts so much, and I want to make sure I'm reading this whole thing right.

"What, you think he stopped climbing? You think he stopped using you to pull himself up?"

All I can do is blink at her. "How are you—how are you okay?"

Her hand comes towards me slowly—telegraphing the motion. She pinches the curve of my ear between two fingers, and it's enough for me to understand: the cybernetics. "Quigley did yours," she says. "Lowell did mine. There's a lot *you* can't do."

"But you're—but we're—"

"Ex*actly*, sweetheart." She lets go of my ear, trails her fingertip over the thin skin behind it. "Remind me, what's your mission?"

My mouth is as dry as if I've eaten paper when I say, "To stop Prime. To kill her. To save the world."

She laughs at a joke I'm not in on.

"Who are you?" I ask, fighting to steady my voice.

"I'm you," she says. "I'm Lowell. Sweetheart, I'm Prime."

So of course I try to kill her, and of course she jumps before she lets me succeed. It's messy, and the mess is in *my room* of all places. I feel sick and it's not just the aftereffects of the distortion.

Wrong-footed from the start. Prime knows we're after her, and she knows just how stupid I'm capable of being.

She knows too much.

There is no way we win this.

Quigley left us, and he trusted us, and I ruined it as soon as I opened my mouth.

AFTER I'VE BURIED the body and showered off, I'm the one crawling into Isadora's bed.

Her room is just as plain as mine: a double bed covered by a blue quilt and gray sheets, a yellow armchair next to a narrow window. I think about waking her up, if only to ask her to move over so that she's not laying diagonally across the mattress. I don't. I make myself as small as I possibly can and deposit myself on top of the quilt.

She knows. She has to know.

But she doesn't know that *I* know.

I'm not going to tip my hand. Not until I have some kind of plan to fix what I've broken, to get the truth out of her and out of my double. To get the truth out of *Prime*.

The fight we're here to stop—it has something to do with the potentials. The cybernetics. The shape of it is still hazy. What is Prime going to do? What are we trying to prevent, and for who?

Whose world are we saving?

I'm no good at this.

My thoughts chase me in circles until the sun comes up. The morning light is much brighter in Isadora's room than in mine, even with the blinds drawn.

When she wakes, she sounds like she's dying in reverse: a wet sort of gasp that reminds me of that last, reflexive breath. Her eyes come open all at once. She barely looks at me. "Pancakes again?" she asks.

chapter
NINE

FTER BREAKFAST, I corner Isadora in the kitchen. "I don't care that the other you will be angry that you were honest," I say, "and you can't up and kill yourself just because I've asked the question."

She drops the soapy sponge she's holding into the sink. She's in charge of dishes, ever since I fucked up Quigley's cast-iron skillet. "Fine. Ask."

"What, exactly, are we stopping Prime from doing?"

She picks up the sponge again, runs it over the blade of a paring knife. "Destroying the Agency."

"How does she do it?"

She rinses the knife, tucks it into the drying rack, pulls her lower lip between her teeth. "Hmm. Well."

"Well?"

"*Quigley* told me not to tell you."

He lied to me, and she's in on it.

Good fathers lie, don't they? Good sisters, on the other hand…I'm not so sure.

"Does this have to do with why the other you is so mean to me?" I ask instead.

"It's like I said. I couldn't kill you if I wasn't, and I've gotten very good at killing you." Isadora pulls the stopper from the sink and wrings out the sponge.

"Not anymore, right?" I push. "Not *this* you. *This* you loves me. You're my sister."

Isadora's words are almost lost under the glug of water in the drain. I've never heard her so unsure, and maybe that means she's being honest. "I have to act mean to *be* mean, and act nice to *be* nice, and it's never much mattered to me which face I'm putting on. Do you understand?"

"I—"

"I don't say this to hurt you," she says, her voice coming out louder. "I just need you to know. It doesn't come naturally to me, any of it. Every kind deed I've done in the past ten months? It's been a choice. You are a choice that I keep making."

"Are you going to keep choosing me?" I ask, and it's my turn to sound too quiet, unsure.

Isadora smiles. "Well, we're sisters, aren't we?"

"You still haven't answered my question."

"*Yes*, Aster, I'll keep choosing you."

"No, before that. *How* does Prime—how does she do it?"

"Hmm," she says again. "Why don't we go sit down?"

AT THE DINING table, Isadora fidgets with Quigley's placemat. There's a science to it, she explains. It's not random. The Agency respects human life far too much to leave something like this to chance.

"Science isn't the same as ethics," I say. She deflects.

There's a…system. Teams of analysts—Quigley used to be one of them—who monitor the timeline for anomalies. Analysts who look for where crimes are likely to be committed, and who's likely to commit them. Analysts who decide who's a potential criminal, then sentence them to die.

"They're slaughtering originals," I say, thinking of the zines. Names and faces. Elders. Children.

Isadora says that it's a mercy, to end their lives before they could harm anyone else. To end lives that probably wouldn't mean anything, anyway. "How many times have you killed me?" she asks. "That's not *actually* murder, and this is no different. Maybe, if it were different, I'd understand why—"

"*How* can you say it's not different?"

I see, then, that this is why Quigley didn't want me to know. Because we have our old selves' personalities and proclivities, and I'm like her, because I *am* her. There was never any way for me to know the truth and still be on his side.

Whose world am I saving, really?

Not his, and not the Agency's.

"Even if it were remotely fair to punish people *before* they commit a crime, how do you know for sure that you've gotten the right people? There has to be some element of profiling, or—"

She pinches the edge of his placemat between her fingers. "He *promised*," she says, her voice all soft again. "It doesn't matter how you feel about it. Quigley promised me that I'd have a life, and I intend to collect."

"How does she do it?" I ask Isadora. "Prime. She fucks the Agency over, but *how*?"

Isadora touches her ear, like she doesn't even know she's doing it. "I don't know." I can't tell if she's lying.

She explains that Quigley made us to preserve the status quo, the balance of power by which the Agency can use TimeFax and no one else can. Putting the TimeFax dupe in Prime's head wasn't a mistake, see, but an experiment. "Imagine if *every* high-level Agency operative could have what we have. Their productivity would skyrocket." And surely Quigley's innovativeness would be rewarded. Surely the inventor of such useful technology would become terribly influential amongst the Agency higher-ups. But Quigley didn't get to *finish* his experiment before Prime hopped off to the future.

It's my turn to say, "Hmm," for two reasons. The first is that it's a bit sad, isn't it, that he's gone so far in search of recognition? The second is that I can see how the implants would level the playing field, if the potentials had access to them: it's impossible to fight back against assassins who can track you anywhere, across space and time. With the ability to jump, they could escape.

But then they'd always be on the run, and a life lived for one purpose is hardly a life at all.

"They deserve better," I say.

Isadora gets up and walks away. She returns hours later, smelling of smoke.

It's NOT A memory, exactly, but a familiar feeling. I feel how Lowell must have felt: so angry it makes my hands itch, but every bit as steady as a sniper. A crystalline awareness of the problem, and a willingness to wait for the perfect solution.

I wait for Prime to come back. Wait for the moment when I can tell her: *Look. I get it now. I see.*

She operates on her own schedule. It's three long weeks before I see her again, and we are running out of time.

"ARE YOU GOING to kill me again?" Prime asks. She's caught me in the basement, exercising to pass the slow afternoon.

"I'd rather let you take care of it."

I've been thinking about what to do with this version of Isadora. She'll need to die a few days early, in case the other Isa is ahead of schedule. I've calculated the time range in which she's likely to arrive, based on the error of her past jumps. Soon.

I don't know what I'll do with Quigley Jr., or her cigar paraphernalia, or all the crime drama tropes I've internalized. I don't know what I'll do without her.

"First," she says, then breathes in like she's winding up for a ramble.

I turn toward her, wince, cut her off: "You don't have to convince me." It will be a matter of convincing Isadora— the real version of her, with the mean twist to her mouth and an insult always held behind her teeth.

Prime smiles like I've surprised her, like she's trying not to show it. "Your sister?" she asks.

"I'll handle it. But I can't—nothing can happen to her, you understand? I'm lost without her." She's my anchor, my tether. If it comes down to it, I'll always choose her.

Prime shrugs, a smooth ripple. "So, you're going to convince her, but you don't want to tip your hand."

"She *can't* know."

"When's this iteration's expiration date?"

"Less than a week, now. Will I…see you again? Before? Before."

That surprised smile again. "You'll see me when it's time." Her smile fades. "Whose world are you saving?" she asks, and I know it's a test.

"Everyone who's been told that their life is worth nothing? Theirs," I say.

"Sweetheart," Prime says, and it comes out terribly fond. "Alright. We're in business."

ON MY LAST night with Isadora, we're watching NCIS in Quigley's bed with her feet resting in my lap. Isadora turns the TV down and says, "I lied to you. Don't tell the other me that I'm telling you this."

"What?"

"I don't want to die with it on my heart."

"Uh, okay. What's wrong?"

"I didn't make you beg to be put down."

I laugh, even though it's not funny. That was so long ago. "I didn't think you did."

"Do you forgive me?"

"Isa, it's really not the biggest deal." I put my hand on hers. "It's fine. It's forgiven."

She's chewing on the inside of her lip, so I know she has more to say. I leave the television volume down low and wait, only halfway watching the unfolding plot.

"I really love Quigley," she says.

"I know." I do too, even though that love has gone complicated.

She turns towards me, folding her legs underneath herself. "I wouldn't save them," she says. "Nothing like that. I'd sooner give them the tools to save themselves."

I turn the TV back up. It might be the most honest thing she's ever said, and she's only said it because she knows she'll never have to own up to it.

Three days later, the real Isadora reappears in the garage, thirty-nine minutes late, with her mouth screwed up in anger again, and all that friendship evaporates.

She looks at me like she'd amputate all four of my limbs and watch me bleed to death, if given the chance—and she probably has. It is such a shame, having seen Isadora's capacity for kindness, to be forced to live with this willfully terrible version of her.

We keep practicing. I keep my cards close to my chest. Prime stays away. I have no idea how to get through to Isadora, but I keep turning over all the things she said during that private, quiet year. Wondering how much of it is still true.

Our jumps get better, then better than that, and it's time to turn our attention to the real job. Quigley is waiting for us—eighteen years from now.

chapter
TEN

IN EIGHTEEN YEARS, Quigley's house outside of Los Angeles still stands, relatively unchanged. We jump together, my hand on Isadora's shoulder, and I land in the garage seven seconds before her with my arm outstretched. There is no one timing me to say I was accurate, but I can tell by the thin blue light cutting through the high windows that I was close enough—it is a winter evening. I wonder if all of our skeletons are still buried in the sprawling yard, all of our ashes scattered to the grass and the transplanted trees.

Quigley isn't waiting for us. I halfway expected him to be here, in his chair in the corner, chewing his thumbnail. I have to remind myself that I *do* still miss him—and there's so much I want to know, from him.

But like I've said, we're the cops. We're the cleanup crew, and Isadora? This version of her? Has no idea that I'm planning to throw her over.

Though Quigley's not here to greet us, he's left us everything we should need, starting with two manila folders on the kitchen table. Isadora picks up the one labeled with her name. A plastic remote the size of a car key slides out from between the pages inside, clattering against the tabletop.

"That's…it?" I ask. The detonator, the artifact that Quigley hopped off to the future to make for us. Fifty-two years ago, the requisite tools to build it didn't exist yet; looking at it, I can't fathom what those tools might be.

"Yep." Isadora thumbs through the folder's contents before she gives me the short of it: tonight, our cleanup duties will take us to Disorder, an upscale casino in the city, where we'll have a chance to corner Prime.

UNLIKE ISADORA'S FOLDER, mine contains only a single sheet of paper with a few handwritten lines: *Protein bars in the cabinet. Clothes upstairs. Listen to your sister.*

Quigley's handwriting strikes me as an odd thing to have missed, and I *must* have missed it, because why else would such a useless note leave me feeling relieved?

I eat two protein bars, shower, and struggle into the dress Quigley's left hanging from my bedroom doorframe. The silver-gray chiffon makes me look like a bridesmaid— but he's also left me a thigh holster, and I don't think all that many bridesmaids are carrying.

When I've given up on twisting my upper body into a pretzel, I open the bedroom door to find Isadora already in the hallway, dressed in a slim-lapeled black suit with the top buttons of the shirt undone. She zips me up.

I start to tell her that she looks nice, but I think of all the ways she could twist it around into an insult and I don't.

The light over the basement steps has burned out. Dust stings my sinuses as I pick my way down the stairs to the gun safe in the dark; after the urge to sneeze comes a stale, heavy smell—which could be anything, with how poorly Quigley's looked after the place. Whatever it is, it's not a priority at present.

Still, curiosity drives me to look closer. The same curiosity, I think, that made me so honest with Prime. It's always been my undoing.

I turn on the overhead light.

The metal folding chair from the garage—the one Quigley used to sit in, when he timed us.

The metal folding chair and *Quigley*, his feet bound to the chair legs, his chest torn open with bullet wounds.

My first thought is that he's seen me dead so many times, but I never expected to see *him* this way. My second thought is that this has Prime's fingerprints all over it, and it's the second thought that matters in a situation like this. My third thought is static, a wide-open and numbed out sort of feeling.

This can't be happening right now. I can't deal with this right now.

But it's already happened. Staring at the wrongness of his body, feet bloated and discolored where the blood's pooled, won't change that.

I turn the light off, holster the pistol, and go find Isadora.

Isadora calls us a car, and I can't resist the impulse to press my hands to the tinted window, my whole body turned and facing out at the passing sights as we head into the city. This body knew the landscape the way it used to be, but to my mind it's all brand new. I have never seen anything quite like this: the streets wreathed in light, the passing cars low and sleek, billboards casting electronic splashes of color over the freeway. We hit traffic and slow to a near halt, and half of me is worried about running behind schedule but the other half of me is grateful to have more time to just look at everything.

Isadora is entirely uninterested, or at least acting like it. She watches the seconds tick by on her watch. She drums her fingers on the leather seat between us.

"Nervous?" I ask. I am thinking of the kinder version of her, the woman I spent a year watching crime dramas with, the woman who doesn't entirely believe in this fight. She's acting mean, because that's what it takes for her to *be* mean. To Prime, to me—it doesn't matter.

"Just want it over with," she says.

"We'll be in and out," I tell her.

Isadora makes a frustrated sound. "I can only hope so."

"It'll be just like Quigley planned it."

She makes that frustrated sound again. I go back to staring out the window.

DISORDER IS THE bottom floor of a posh Westside hotel, all plush red carpet and years of layered perfume. The waitresses all look alike, so that it is the same woman who offers to take our coats and brings us flutes of champagne and clips the end of Isadora's cigar. It takes me too long to realize that she's a hologram created by a cluster of drones moving in sync. I tell Isa. She checks her watch.

"Quigley said Prime would be in the east bathroom at 9:57 pm," she says.

"We're cornering her in the bathroom?" I should've tried to steal her folder while she was showering, though I doubt I'd have gotten away with it.

"Do you have a better idea?"

I blink. Her cigar smoke is irritating my eyes and, even worse, she's gonna make me smell like an ashtray.

"It's not likely to be crowded. It's not likely to cause a scene," Isadora says. She touches her jacket pocket. Must be where she's keeping the detonator.

"Fine," I say. "We have fifteen minutes."

"That's an approximation," she says, looking down at her watch. "We can't afford to be approximate."

"Shut up and finish your cigar," I tell her.

Thirteen minutes later we are sitting in a cluster of lounge chairs opposite the restroom door. "You know what she looks like?" I ask Isadora, and she nods as if it's obvious.

The holographic waitress passes, carrying a tray of drinks, and Prime appears from behind her. She's wearing a different dress but she has my face, my hair, my way of holding her hands as if she's afraid to get them dirty. When the distortion hits, I'm ready for it.

I look from her to Isadora, waiting for the moment to break. Her gaze is pointed steadily at the ashtray. "Let's go," she says.

"Were you ever going to tell me?"

"Aster, let's *go*. Time's short, and we've got a vagabond to kill."

"Was *any* iteration of you *ever* going to tell me?"

Her mouth twists. "She's you—and I know how to kill you. I'm quite good at killing you."

"Just tell me—when did he tell you?"

Isadora shrugs in the way that I hate. "I guessed. Quigley told me to make myself an expert in your body. I had a hard time figuring out what he meant, at first—he wanted an expert in taking you apart."

What gets to me isn't the lying, because I knew she was lying, because I always expect her to lie. What gets to me is the blatant lack of remorse, even now. "When all this is over," I say, "I might just kill you for good."

"I dare you to try."

And then—horror of horrors—Isadora winks at me. She abandons her cigar in the ashtray and makes for the bathroom door.

chapter
ELEVEN

THE TUG OF distortion makes me overly aware of my hands as we walk into the women's restroom, the way I hold them in front of my chest instead of letting my arms fall limp at my sides. The way Prime holds herself.

The restroom has a lounge area with mirrors ringed with lightbulbs and purple wingback chairs; past that there's a doorway to an area with stalls and sinks. A toilet flushes. A stall door creaks open. My hand goes to the pistol under my dress.

A blonde woman comes out, smoothing down the front of her red gown. She only halfway washes her hands, then checks her teeth in the mirror and bustles past us. I can hardly breathe, for the anticipation and the pain—for the anticipation *of* pain.

Then the farthest stall opens, and Prime comes out. She looks at us like she's fighting the urge to roll her

eyes. "Look, I don't want to hurt you," she says. I look at
Isadora, at Prime, at Isadora again. When I turn back
Isadora has a machete in her hand—where the fuck did
she get a machete?

Prime groans. Her eyes flash. I start counting the
seconds in my head, *one-Mississippi* like I'm a child.

Isadora raises the machete, and then there is another
Prime materializing and charging at her, stance low, arms
around Isadora's middle like a football player.

"I said," says Prime, "that I don't want to hurt you."

I reach for the gun.

Isa lands flat on her back on the tile floor with an *oof*
sound as the weight of the woman on top of her pushes the
air out of her lungs. She drops the machete, then swings
with her whole body and punches Prime's duplicate
across the face. Her head snaps back, blood from her nose
staining the front of Isadora's suit.

Isadora picks up the machete and buries it in Prime's
double's side, then pulls it back out in a spray of blood. I
feel like I am seeing my own guts. I wonder if this is why
Isadora let me see her torturing my doubles so often—
so that I would be ready, unfazed by violence done to
bodies that look identical to my own, by the way temporal
distortion makes the edges of my vision darken and blur.
It was all part of Quigley's design, and she *lied* to me, and
steadily kept on lying.

I would tell her everything—every awful thing, every
secret from that invisible year—if she'd be honest with me
for just a second.

The hate for her that grows in my chest is pressing on
my heart, muffling its beating.

All I can feel are my hands, both curled around the
warm metal of the gun, which is steadily aimed at Prime's
center of mass. "Don't do that again," I tell her, then
curse myself for how imbecilic that sounds. I'm in a casino
bathroom pointing a gun at a woman who looks exactly

like me, while Isadora squirms out from under Prime's double's dying body; I wish I had something clever to say.

"Isa?"

"Yeah?"

"Detonate." If it works like Quigley said it would, it'll emit a frequency that shuts down Prime's implant and renders her temporarily normal, useless, unable to jump. It will also do the same to us.

Isadora shakes her head. "Not yet." Her eyes flash. "Let's keep doing this the hard way. It's kinda fun, right?"

"Not for me."

"You don't know what you're doing," Prime says, and I'm wondering if—when—to give the game away.

Isadora laughs. Her eyes flash again. I start counting the seconds. I get to three before two copies of Isadora appear behind Prime, one of them reaching to restrain each side of her body.

Prime doesn't even struggle. "You know I can just keep jumping, right?" she asks.

"Fine. I'm quite enjoying myself, if you hadn't noticed. I'll just keep killing you."

"Give it a second," Prime says. "Look, I don't know what happens in the middle, but I've seen how all this ends. I need you to trust me."

Isadora makes a sound, face contorting—distortion setting in. I see an opening. I calibrate for the smallest increment of time that I can. I jump.

IT IS LESS than a second later and I am reaching into Isadora's pocket for the detonator, pressing the button before she can swing her elbow back into my face. The machete slides into my chest sharp as a song. I think of what Isa would say.

You can tolerate pain, and it's not like you're really dying. You have nothing to be afraid of.

I AM SHAKING as my duplicate falls to the ground, chest carved open with a single swing of the blade. Isadora spits at the writhing body. My ears are ringing fiercely.

"Fuck you," Isadora says, to the version of me that has just laid her low.

"How does it end?" I ask Prime.

"The three of us," she says. "No Quigley. No Agency bullshit. The three of us in the farmhouse, having changed the world."

"We give them the tools to save themselves?" I ask. I don't know if this version of Isadora will recognize the words, but I have hope.

Isadora curses again, spits again, but when I look at her she's sheathing the machete.

"We do," Prime says. "And besides, if you kill me, you'll never know what happened to Quigley."

WE LEAVE THE four corpses behind in their respective smears of gore—one of Prime, one of me, two of Isadora. Isadora takes off her ruined shirt and shoves it into the bathroom garbage can, then wraps herself in her black suit jacket, its dark color hiding the bloodstains. I keep a hand on Prime's arm as the holographic waitress calls us a car, a driverless pod with two bench seats. Prime sits sandwiched between me and Isadora. My skin prickles everywhere we're touching.

Isadora inputs the address of the farmhouse.

"If I may—" Prime starts to say.

"You may *not*," Isadora interrupts.

"Go ahead," I say.

Prime commandeers the dashboard display and types out a different address—one I don't recognize. "We have to go back," she says. "We'll need a TimeFax machine for that, won't we? I know where we can find one."

THE AGENCY CAMPUS in Santa Monica could be anything, in the dark: a college, a hospital, a military base, an outpost of an overpowered law enforcement bureau. It's a cluster of beige buildings lit by floodlights, connected by gritty concrete walkways with bits of sagebrush planted along their edges. The air smells of sand, and this is as cold as LA gets, and I'm glad I wore flats because Prime is practically running.

She punches a code into a keypad and there's the *whir-click* of an electronic lock releasing, and then we could be in any office building. It's as nondescript as the set of a television show. Carpet, cubicles, ergonomic rolling chairs.

"Come on," Prime says.

It's so…banal. Hard to believe that so much power comes from such a boring place.

The TimeFax machines are kept in a back room, five of them in a row packed in along with a laser printer and a lamination machine. My hands feel itchy seeing them—watching Prime look them over—but she begins to type coordinates first into one, then another.

"Same location," she says. "Twenty-four hours back. The building will be empty, we'll get a cab to the farmhouse—easy money." She waves a hand towards Isadora, beckoning. "Put your hands on the machine. This one's yours."

"How do I know you won't—" Isadora starts.

"Come on, look at the coordinates. You'll be the one to push the button, alright?"

Isadora looks at me before she steps closer to the TimeFax machine, and for a moment it's like I'm looking at that scared, kind version of her. I'm thinking of her with swollen eyes and messy hair, crawling into my bed. *Come on, if you're coming.*

"Go on," I say, all instinct.

Her mouth goes angry again, and I see the moment it happens, how she *decides* to put it on. "Like I need you to tell me what to do," she says. Her eyes skim over the coordinates, and then she knocks the side of her fist into the *START* button and rests both of her hands on the sensors on the top of the machine. The whole apparatus gives a low beep.

"That's…it?" I don't know what I expected.

"You next," Prime says. "Once we've all jumped, I'll take you across the campus to the disposal building."

"You next," I echo, mirroring her little *go ahead* gesture. She's me, and she knows she's being mocked, and she hates it.

"Fine." She presses the button, brings her hands down on the top of the machine. It beeps. "Your turn."

I enter the coordinates myself, Prime watching from just behind me. With my hands on the sensors, the beep echoes through my bones like they're tuning forks. I squeeze my eyes shut, and then I'm in the past.

chapter
TWELVE

IT'S TWENTY-FOUR HOURS earlier and I'm *angry*.

Angry at myself, that I land looking around for Isadora.

Angry at Isadora, for…everything.

She blinks at me, her face drawn and disoriented, and it comes out: "You were a good sister to me for *a whole fucking year*. There is no reason—no reason!—for you to be so awful all the time."

"Where's Prime?" she asks.

"Like I give a single fuck about Prime!" Wait. I give myself longer than a microsecond to think about what she's said, about the fact that Prime isn't in this little workroom with us. "Where's Prime?"

"A whole year?" Isadora asks.

"Fuck off and die," I say.

"A whole year." The set of her jaw shifts, then relaxes.

"What did I tell you?"

"Does it matter, now?"

"It was Quigley—who told me not to. Told me to keep things from you, or else you'd become just like her."

"Too late."

"She's going to—"

"Save the world," I say. "What Quigley made us for? It was a heap of shit, but what *she's* doing—she's actually going to change things for the better. It just took me a long time to see the shape of it."

Isadora heaves herself up so that she's sitting on top of the TimeFax machine. *That's a dangerous piece of equipment worth millions of dollars*, I want to say. I don't.

"All Quigley wanted was power," she says. "And it *does* matter, Aster, because whatever that other me *didn't* tell you? I'll tell you now. I'll tell you the whole story right now."

"What about Prime?"

"You watched her type in the coordinates, didn't you? She'll be here."

"SHE WAS A researcher," Isadora says. "He was her… intern? Her assistant. She was this big-shot Agency researcher and he did little stuff. Got her coffee, transcribed her notes, put down her doubles."

"And the two of them were—"

"Under the table. They couldn't have worked together if anyone knew, you know?"

"And she was—"

That's when Prime comes in and Isadora says, "Where the fuck were you?"

"Evidence." She holds up a flash drive, then tucks it away. "Who was Lowell? You want to play ball, come on—let's play ball."

WHO WAS LOWELL? In short, she was a genius.

To tell the whole truth, she was neurotic about mess—everything had to be *just so*. She hated to get her hands dirty unless it was for a good reason. She thought kissing was the height of physical comedy. She wanted so badly to be loved that she thought Quigley loved her. She wanted so badly to love that she thought she loved *him*, and maybe that's even worse.

She could be quiet about her beliefs, but the truth would bleed out one way or another: in words, in deeds, sometimes subtle and sometimes bold. She understood the value in playing along until it was time to make a break. She knew how to change a system from the inside, how to take root like a virus and spread.

Designing the cybernetics was her most blatant act of defiance, and she died for it.

She built the TimeFax implants with Agency resources, but she didn't build them *for* the Agency. She cobbled them together on her own time, in stolen overtime hours. She built them out of spite. She built them because she knew what the Agency was headed toward, and she wanted to give everyone it would mow down the means to fight back. TimeFax without access to a TimeFax machine? That was a revolutionary prospect. One that could change the tide for the underdog.

Quigley played along, pretended to align himself with Lowell's cause, but when the cybernetics were nearly complete, he killed her and put her on ice, the way the Agency tended to freeze a few doubles of every employee. He turned her in as an insurgent, thinking he'd be lauded as a hero.

The higher-ups spared half a second for Quigley's story. "Alright, buddy boy," the bosses said, "if the cybernetics would be so dangerous in the wrong hands, why don't you finish building them—for us? Maybe then, you can run with the big dogs."

So Quigley set to work trying to finish the cybernetics that Lowell had nearly perfected. He never quite nailed the finer details—backwards travel, preventing temporal distortion—but they worked well enough. The Agency sabotaged him at every turn, denying his requests for equipment and frozen bodies. He knew he'd been set up to fail, and he knew he wouldn't fail upwards. He didn't have Lowell's propensity for stealing from the corporate overlords. Even when he was got close to a breakthrough, he was running out of corpses to experiment on.

Which is why, after a few months on ice, he brought Lowell back to life. She was the same woman, with the same core drives, but she'd lost half of her memory and the rest was all scrambled. Quigley called her Prime.

Isadora shrugs, her hands splayed out. "Mindless corporate drone in more trouble than he knows how to handle."

Prime says, "All he ever wanted was to climb, and he was going to use *you* to do it. Every single version of you."

"But you got to me first."

"I always will," Prime says.

She's been kicking around the timeline for so much longer than me, racking up years of experience, aided by cybernetics that can do *more* than mine. She's who I could be—who I *will* be. A stronger, smarter version of me.

She was always going to get to me. She was always going to change me. She was always going to win me over.

And Isadora? I was always going to win her over, too.

"If I was Lowell, who were you?" I ask her.

Isadora makes that sour face again, and I know it was the wrong question. "You think that wasn't the first thing I asked him, after he told me about you? I was nobody," she says. "A junior analyst. But he told me—he promised that I could *be* someone, after this was all over."

Prime beats me to the punch: "So, he brought you back from the dead into a life you never wanted. That doesn't mean it's not worth living."

"I tried to be so good for him," Isadora whispers. "I did everything he wanted."

"What will you do now?" Prime asks.

Isadora breathes in, rolls her shoulders back. "I'll figure it out," she says.

chapter
THIRTEEN

QUIGLEY'S TIED TO a chair under the basement stairs—alive, mercifully, though he's seen better days. I hate the part of me that wants to undo the knots holding him in place, whispering, *Father, father, let me help you. Tell me how to help you. Help me to help you.*

When the light comes on it's triumph in his eyes, seeing us: his weapons, and his target. He moves his chapped lips around the filthy bandana he's gagged with. Under his gaze, I give in. He tilts his head down and I reach around him to untie the gag.

"Water," he says.

"Water," I say to Prime.

"Go get him water," Prime says to Isadora.

"Fuck you," says Isadora, but she goes.

I look at Prime, look at Quigley, see him register the

way my eyes slide back and forth. See his confusion. "Father," I say, and it's every part of speech, every word I don't have it in me to say.

Isadora comes back with a full glass. I hold it to Quigley's mouth without untying his hands or feet.

"Father," Isadora says, her voice a weapon and a wound. "You are so fucking unoriginal. You know, I never really thought about how stupid you must be? You brought back Lowell, who you *knew* wouldn't want shit to do with you after you *killed* her, and then you brought back one of her doubles to try and find her? And stuck me right in the middle of it?"

"No," I say. "It was smart. It was stupid, but it was smart, too."

Prime nods towards me. "She's right."

"Isa knows how to kill Prime because she knows how to kill *me*, but I know how she thinks."

Quigley's mouth falls open, then slams shut like he's trying to win back his lost dignity. "How?"

"You were working with incomplete schematics, but I knew the rest," Prime says. "Backwards travel. A cure for distortion. All of that was in *me*, and you never stood a chance."

He looks like he's going to cry, and I can't take it. I squint at my own hands around the glass of water, the stained concrete floor refracted through it.

"If I recall correctly, you were a fantastic assistant, right up until you killed me," Prime says. I can't get past the feeling that I'm looking at a photograph of myself. I look at her for a long time and notice that the pain of it's been shrinking, like the old ache in my knee. Easy to ignore.

Prime meets my gaze. "You've seen how this ends. Get on with it."

I hand her the glass of water and reach under my dress for the gun. I go to my knees, then. "You truly were a shit father," I tell him.

He pushes his shoulder forward, like he wants to rest his

bound hand on my bowed head. "Oh, my love. It doesn't have to be like this." His voice gives out.

I don't know why I feel like crying. Quigley was terrible to me, to Lowell, to Prime, to Isadora. It's like Isa said: he's a mindless Agency drone in more trouble than he can handle, more interested in maintaining the balance of power than anything. He would do anything to climb within a system that doesn't care about him at all.

I don't apologize before I rise to my feet and shoot him in the chest.

THE THREE OF us walk out to the pine trees at the property line, sit among their roots in our fancy clothes. Isadora apologizes for trying to kill Prime, and Prime laughs with how unexpected it is. Isadora doesn't apologize for the violence she committed against me, but I don't especially need her to. I understand why she did it—for Quigley, for his ideals, because it was what she was resurrected to do.

"How does it end?" I ask Prime.

"We sit here for a while," she says. "There will be a version of me that needs to see this."

So, we talk. For hours, we commiserate about Quigley and learning to jump to the future and killing our doubles. We discuss our favorite murder weapons and disposal methods. I tell Prime how Isadora butchered me again and again, at Quigley's orders. I tell her everything.

"What comes next?" I ask, once Prime's explained how she installed her own cybernetics. "We give them to the potentials, right? The implants?"

She looks at me, then snorts. "I'm going to blame that bit of stupidity on the ice," she says.

"I don't think it's stupid," Isadora says. "Isn't that what Lowell wanted, originally?

"Yeah, but everything's a nail to a hammer." Prime

leans back on her hands, makes that face like she's trying not to roll her eyes—I can't make it out that well in the dark, but I can imagine. "Let's say you've got an army of fascists with guns. Is the most efficient way to stop them to give their victims guns, too? Or do you take their guns away altogether?"

"Huh," Isadora says, like hearing it so bluntly has her stunned.

"I only waited so long so that you'd get *better*. I had to know that you were precise enough."

That explains the long months of torment, the way Prime took her time feeling me out, even though it must've been one very long day for her.

"Do you see it, now? We're going to destroy every single TimeFax machine—*at the same time*."

Prime lets us sit with that for a while, and I halfway expect Isadora to object. I want to tell her that she can still be someone—live a life worth having—even outside of the framework she was taught to look for meaning within. I think she already knows. I think she's known all along, but was scared to really see it.

The night's gone dark and starry when Prime says, "Look," and a version of her—navy blue coveralls, hair pulled into two buns—appears just beyond the property line. Prime stands up, waves, walks towards her. The two of them stand together and talk for a long time, voices too quiet to make out at this distance.

"That's how I first saw her," I tell Isadora. "That year. That whole year, that was how I saw her."

"I can't imagine. A year's such a long time."

"Well, it was three hundred and sixty-two days."

Her startled laughter tapers off into a sigh. "And it really wasn't terrible?"

I want to tell her about the heist movies and police procedurals, her sourdough starter, her box of cigars. How infuriating she could be, in entirely mundane ways.

How kind she could be, when she had nothing to lose.

Instead, I say, "I would do it again."

She squeezes my hand. "Let's get through tonight, first."

Prime hugs her double, kisses the corner of her mouth, tips her head back and laughs long and loud. When she turns back towards me and Isadora, the double pulls out a gun and shoots herself through the temple.

Prime doesn't flinch at the shot. She throws herself down at the base of a tree. "I've told her everything," she says. "It's all in motion, now." When she smiles, I almost don't recognize the expression for its wickedness. "You think the detonator's worn off by now? Let's go ruin the Agency. Let's go *save the world*."

ACKNOWLEDGMENTS

Thank you to the Bicoastal Writers Workshop—C. J. Linton, Rachel Linton, Rien Hu, and Renee Scavone—for reading countless drafts of this story before I even knew what it was. You asked all the right questions and pushed me in all the right directions. C. J., thank you for seeing the story I wanted to write, the story I'd written, and the gaps between the two. Rachel, thank you for the many discussions of the mechanisms of fascism. Rien, thank you for the phone call where we cracked Isadora's motivations. And Renee, thank you for loving R&P so loudly even when it felt like a handful of wet spaghetti; your relentless faith in my ability to see this through was transformative. I truly cannot believe you all were willing to read so many versions of the pocket year.

Thank you to dave ring for your friendship, editorial guidance, and friendship again. Thank you to Jordan Shiveley for designing the cover of my dreams, and thank you to Sarah Gailey for hosting my dream cover reveal.

I am forever grateful to the family that grew me (all fifty 'leven of you). Thank you to my grandmother, Hazel Greene, who transcribed stories for me before I could hold a pen. Thank you to my mother, Karla Greene, who—among so very many things—indulged my childhood fascination with fax machines.

Thank you to the family that chose me, that keeps choosing me. Thank you to Charlie, Liz, Sam, Car, and Dmitrii for every rambling phone call, every flurry of all-caps messages, every podcast-length voice memo. You all keep me going. I hope I've done you proud.

And lastly, thank you to my friends in the pub. Next round's on me.

ABOUT THE AUTHOR

Dominique Dickey is a speculative fiction writer and game designer. As the creative director of Sly Robot Games, they've created *Plant Girl Game* and *Tomorrow on Revelation III*. They contributed to the Nebula Award-winning *Thirsty Sword Lesbians*, and the ENNIE Award-winning *Journeys Through the Radiant Citadel*. Their short fiction has appeared in venues including *Fantasy Magazine*, *Lightspeed Magazine*, and *Nightmare Magazine*. They live in the DC area, where they're always on the hunt for their next idea. You can find their work at dominiquedickey.com.

ABOUT THE PRESS

Neon Hemlock is a Washington, DC-based small press publishing speculative fiction, rad zines, and queer chapbooks. Publishers Weekly once called us "the apex of queer speculative fiction publishing" and we're still beaming. Learn more about us at neonhemlock.com and on social medias at @neonhemlock.

www.ingramcontent.com/pod-product-compliance
Lightning Source LLC
Chambersburg PA
CBHW031357060726
47590CB00007B/2832